It's time to Stand Up and Speak Up!

For Yourself and Others

Written by
Bob Sornson

Author of the award-winning book, *The Juice Box Bully*

Illustrated by Shelley Johannes

FERNE PRESS

It's Time to Stand Up and Speak Up! For Yourself and Others
Copyright © 2014 by Bob Sornson
Layout and cover design by Jacqueline L. Challiss Hill
Illustrations created by Shelley Johannes
Illustrations created with pencil and digital color
Printed in the United States of America

Summary: When Wendy is treated disrespectfully by fellow students, she uses the four steps from the Stand Up, Speak Up program to deal with the situation.

Library of Congress Cataloging-in-Publication Data
Sornson, Bob
It's Time to Stand Up and Speak Up! For Yourself and Others/Bob Sornson–First Edition
ISBN-13: 978-1-938326-15-8
1. Juvenile fiction. 2. Bystanders. 3. Elementary school. 4. Bullying. 5. Respect.
I. Sornson, Bob II. Title
Library of Congress Control Number: 2013949131

FERNE PRESS

Ferne Press is an imprint of Nelson Publishing & Marketing
366 Welch Road, Northville, MI 48167
www.nelsonpublishingandmarketing.com
(248) 735-0418

Our children are growing up in a culture that includes violent videos and games, obscene song lyrics, and political discourse lacking respect and basic courtesy. And yet there are so many homes and classrooms in which adults consistently model and teach respectful behavior and respectful speech. This book is dedicated to the parents and teachers who unfailingly teach children to stand up and speak up for honorable behavior.

"Thanks for holding that open for me,"
Wendy called ahead to Jennifer and Heather.
But the two girls didn't hold the door.

4

They smiled at each other and didn't look back as they walked into school.
The door swung shut before Wendy could reach it.

"Hey, that was rude!" yelled Molly, Wendy's friend.

"Maybe they didn't hear me," Wendy offered.

"I'm going to say something to those girls," Molly said.

"No, thanks," replied Wendy. "I'll let you know if I need some help."

In the hallway before lunch, Wendy saw Jennifer and Heather.

"Want to eat lunch
with us today?"
Jennifer asked.

"Sure, I guess," Wendy replied. "You can come sit at our table."

"Let's just sit by ourselves so we can talk," Jennifer suggested.
Wendy agreed to meet them at the corner table that was usually empty.

Wendy walked through the lunch line with Molly.
"I'll eat with you," said Molly.
"I don't trust those girls. They're sneaky."

"No, thanks," said Wendy.
"I'll be okay."

"If you say so," Molly said.
"Meet you on the
playground
after lunch."

Wendy waited at the table in the corner.

When Jennifer and Heather came into the cafeteria, they began talking with their friends.

Jennifer pointed across the room at Wendy, and the group laughed.

Once she realized what
was happening, Wendy
felt her face get really hot.

She tried to step back,
cool down, and let her anger
and disappointment go.

But it wasn't working.

16

Wendy waved to Molly and her other friends,
and they came marching across the room with their lunch trays.

"They're so mean," Molly yelled. "They shouldn't be laughing at you."

"Step back, Molly," suggested Ben, "and calm down."

18

Surrounded by her friends, Wendy took a deep breath and began to relax.

"Are you okay?" Rosie asked.

"Thanks for coming to help me," Wendy said.
"But I'm calm now. I'm ready to deal with
Jennifer and Heather on my own. And Molly,"
she said as she looked directly at her friend,
"please don't say anything unless I ask."

Wendy led her friends
across the cafeteria.

When they reached the table, everyone was quiet.
Wendy didn't raise her voice.
She didn't look angry.
She spoke with a quiet strength
and looked directly at the girls.

22

"Jennifer and Heather, I guess you didn't really want to have lunch with me.
Your loss. But I don't appreciate it when you try to ridicule me.
I deserve to be treated with as much respect as anyone else.
Please remember that."

"Whatever," Jennifer replied.

She got up from the table and turned to leave.
Heather remained seated.

"Are you coming?" Jennifer demanded.
Heather shook her head and stayed in her seat.
Jennifer walked away.

"I am sorry," Heather said.
"It was mean, and I shouldn't have done that."

25

Wendy sat down next to her.

"I felt badly about what we did but didn't speak up," explained Heather.

"You chose to be a bystander to mean behavior!" Molly interjected.

"What's a bystander?" Heather asked.

"A bystander is someone who watches bad things happen and chooses not to stand up or speak up," Ben explained.

"Oh," said Heather.
"I don't want to be a bystander."

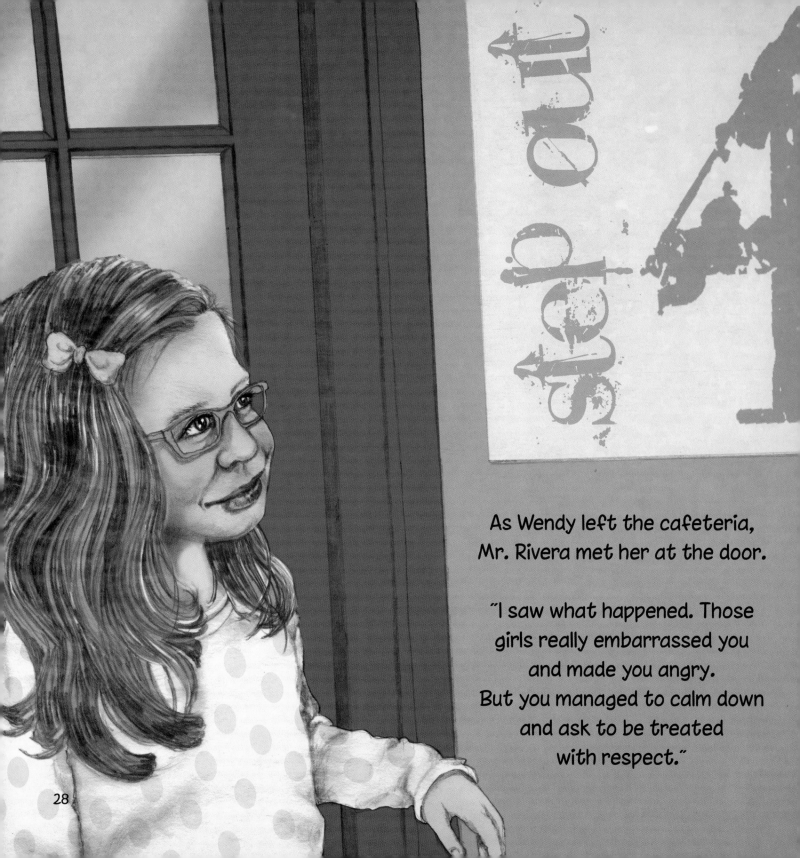

step out

As Wendy left the cafeteria,
Mr. Rivera met her at the door.

"I saw what happened. Those
girls really embarrassed you
and made you angry.
But you managed to calm down
and ask to be treated
with respect."

"Great job standing up
and speaking up for yourself."

"I thought about coming to you
for help," Wendy admitted.
"But after a minute,
I figured I could handle it
on my own."

He smiled. "You sure did."

Dear Reader,

As parents and teachers, it's our responsibility to help our children learn to stand up for themselves and others, speak up when it's safe, and build communities in which we treat each other with respect and dignity.

In this story, Wendy has cerebral palsy, which is a condition that makes the muscles in her arms and legs tight and sometimes shaky. Jennifer's character represents those kids who like to put others down and try to take advantage of those children who might be vulnerable. But Wendy is strong in ways that Jennifer does not fully understand.

We can help our children:

- develop the character and skills to build a social culture in which every person is treated with respect.
- learn that standing by while bad things happen gives permission for cruel behaviors.
- build confidence so they can stand up and speak up for themselves and others.

Whether it's Wendy or her friends, all kids can learn to stand up and speak up for themselves and others.

Bob Sornson

The Stand Up, Speak Up program teaches kids to think about how to treat each other and develop the confidence and the skills needed to stand up and speak up for themselves and others. This program helps children learn to choose not to be bystanders when they see disrespectful behavior. For more information, visit www.no-bystanders.com.

If you are being mistreated, these "Four Steps to Taking Action" will help you.

1. **Step Back:** Take a look at what's going on and calmly decide what to do.
2. **Step In:** If you feel safe, tell that person to stop, or try to move away or ignore.
3. **Step Up:** Ask friends to step up and go with you if you want support.
4. **Step Out:** Talk to an adult if you need help or advice.

If you see the mistreatment of others, learn the "Four Steps to Taking Action."

1. **Step Back:** Look at the situation and decide if someone is being mistreated. Ask yourself if you would like to be treated that way.
2. **Step In:** Don't be a bystander. Ask the person being mistreated if he/she needs help.
3. **Step Up:** Show support if you feel it is safe to do so.
4. **Step Out:** Talk to an adult if you need help or advice.

Author

Bob Sornson, PhD, is the founder of the Early Learning Foundation. He is dedicated to helping schools and parents give every child an opportunity to achieve early learning success. His pre-K to grade 3 Early Learning Success Initiative has demonstrated that we can help many more children become successful learners for life.

Bob is the author of numerous publications. *Fanatically Formative, Successful Learning During the Crucial K-3 Years* (Corwin, 2012), *Creating Classrooms Where Teachers Love to Teach* (Love and Logic Press, 2005), *The Juice Box Bully* (Ferne Press, 2010), and *Stand in My Shoes: Kids Learning about Empathy* (Love and Logic Press, 2013) are among his bestsellers. To contact Bob or learn more about his publications and workshops, please visit www.earlylearningfoundation.com.

Illustrator

Shelley Johannes began her artistic career after ten years in the architectural design industry. While that was fun, she found her dream job when motherhood introduced her to the world of children's books. Five years and a dozen books later, she still pinches herself everyday. A library fanatic who used to walk to the bus stop with her nose in a book, Shelley still reads every chance she gets. Iced cappuccinos and book recommendations are her favorite gifts. When she's not painting or playing with her boys, she writes about her adventures in books at thebookdiariesblog.com. Shelley wishes she could live in perpetual autumn, but for now she lives in Michigan where she enjoys the colorful chaos of life, with her husband, Bob, and their two boys, Matthew and Nolan.